CHARMED BY A SPELL

CANDACE ROBINSON

Cover Design by S.E.D. Creations

For those who wish to dance with a ghost

Thick green smoke curled toward the ceiling out of the cauldron, and a foul odor like rotten eggs invaded Beatrice's nose. She snatched a broomstick in the corner of the cellar, then waved it around in a futile effort to redirect the smoke from reaching the main parts of her home.

"Another failure," she sobbed in frustration and sank down in the chair of her desk. Lifting the jar of bat wings, she rotated the glass around and around. "Did I miscount? Should I have added another?"

The door at the top of the stairs creaked open, and she craned her neck to find her older brother's head protruding through the door.

"Why are you still down there?" Claude shouted, his hair perfectly combed. "You are supposed to be readying yourself for the ball this evening."

"I have more important tasks to complete!" she snapped at him, wiping the tears from her cheeks so he wouldn't see.

"You need to find a husband, *Beatrice*, instead of putting your entire focus on contacting the dead. Now, be ready tonight or else you'll have to deal with Father," he reprimanded before shutting the door with a harsh click.

For the past three years, Beatrice's family had *encouraged* her to begin courting. Her father and brother both acted as though she were an old maid when most women in their village didn't marry until they reached twenty years of age. She had only just turned nineteen last season!

"You're the one who needs to find a wife instead of sticking your cock in any woman who shows you a little attention," Beatrice muttered. "What *I* need to find is a spell that works properly."

Only, she wasn't the strongest witch in North Tarrytown, or Sleepy Hollow, as the story liked to impose. She was perhaps an arm's length from being a mediocre witch. And even that title could only be boasted after using other witches' spells.

However, there were more important matters for her at hand. She stood from the chair and peered down at the murky liquid inside her cauldron. Two weeks had passed since her closest friend's death. She'd cared about Heath more than anyone. He'd made her laugh when she felt no joy—he was the only person who ever understood her, gave her comfort on her best and worst days, and talked her through her frustration at her failing spells.

Beatrice's father had taken him in after the village's blacksmith passed, the last of Heath's blood family. Even if Heath had ventured in from another town, he would've found solace and been welcomed with open arms because of his paranormal ability. Not everyone in North Tarrytown held a unique quality, but those who didn't were sworn to protect their neighbors' secrets from travelers regardless.

Beatrice sighed at her failed brew one more time and grasped her skirts before bounding up the wooden steps. Her mother was most likely in their library reading through an old tome, but Claude stood at the window in the sitting room, peering out at the garden.

She didn't acknowledge him as she reached for the doorknob, and without glancing up from his stoic position, he said, "And where are you off to? If you don't court someone soon, Father has decided you will join the nunnery. You have one month."

Beatrice tightened her fists and pursed her lips. "Then I suppose that means I'm off to tumble someone."

Claude's gaze snapped to hers, his nostrils flaring. "You are driving everyone in this house mad," he said. "All three of our sisters are happily married."

And good for them. They'd wanted to wed. Her sisters were all cat shifters like her mother and father while Claude held a special unicorn shifting ability. Even if Beatrice wasn't the strongest witch, she'd never cared that she wasn't a shifter. There wasn't any other magic they could do besides turn into something non-human.

"I will attend this evening just as you want. Don't you worry about that." With a mocking smile, she opened the door and stepped out into the warm afternoon.

Beatrice passed through the rose gardens, and she held back more tears that threatened to fall when she looked toward Heath's small cottage. Her father had given it to him as soon as he arrived. To keep the property, Heath's duty had been to tend to the crops and animals.

Her father hadn't meant for Beatrice and Heath to become friends, but they were close in age, and she'd grown curious about the mysterious boy who seemed just as alone as she was. When they were younger they would catch frogs together, then play games in the cornfield behind her manor. He was the one person she could confess her secrets to who wouldn't tell anyone else. They vowed to always have each other's backs as long as they lived—a promise, a happiness Beatrice had taken for granted, a friend she'd been so sure would last until she was old and decrepit. But instead, Heath had died, leaving her alone once again.

As she took the winding trail toward Jeanne's home, she could only concentrate on her brother's words. It wasn't an exaggeration—her father would most certainly force her into a nunnery. She'd told him for years that, other than practicing her spells, she wanted to tend to the farm. Her father refused to allow her to dream, calling it a mundane existence, a waste of her talents and beneath his family's reputation.

Beatrice trekked past the rows of ferns and aloe vera in Jeanne's garden to the front door of the woman's cozy cottage. As soon as it was discovered that Beatrice wasn't a shifter but a witch, she'd been placed under the old woman's wing to teach her everything she knew. However, not much had improved—she'd managed to master only the basic spells that almost any witch could perform. None of that had mattered, at least not until she'd lost Heath.

Before Beatrice knocked on the door, Jeanne drew it open, her gray hair in disarray and her wool skirt covered in stains.

"Did you get the spell to work?" the old woman asked, her arms folded.

"Of course not. I tried the spell just as instructed

in the allotted time frame you requested. Please help me this one time," Beatrice begged. She had to know that Heath wasn't trapped in the ghost realm, frequented by the Headless Horseman who took the heads of the dead.

Jeanne didn't easily hand out spells she made, but she was the only witch who would help her.

After a long moment, Jeanne sighed. "This one time. From here on out, I want you to create them on your own." She whirled around, her boots thumping across the wooden floor.

Relief washed over Beatrice when the witch returned with a small jar containing an iridescent liquid that swirled inside the glass.

"What do I owe you for it?" Beatrice asked. Even if the witch required a tooth in exchange, she would pull one out for her.

Jeanne rested her weathered hand on Beatrice's shoulder. "Nothing. I know how much you miss Heath." She placed the jar in her palm. "If you need the spell again, you'll have to create it, understand?"

Beatrice thanked her, then grappling with her skirts, she rushed like a madwoman toward the cemetery up the road. Her conscience had weighed on her since Heath's death, yearning to know that his soul was in Heaven, to say the goodbye she had not been granted. Once she confirmed he was safe, then she would ... what? Find a husband? Go to the nunnery? The thought of several of the older and wealthy men her father would want her to marry made Beatrice's skin crawl.

The wind tousled her hair as she entered the cemetery. She stopped in front of Heath's unmarked grave near the back of the woods. If her parents' wealth belonged to her, she would've had a proper headstone made, but instead she'd nailed two pieces of wood together and placed the cross into the ground for him.

Unfastening the lid of the jar, Beatrice poured the contents onto Heath's grave. She repeated the incantation Jeanne had taught her, and the wind blew harder, her words becoming an echo inside of a blanket of white fog. The spell was *working.*

"Heath, can you hear me?" she shouted. "Are you there?" Silence reigned through the spell, making her heart pound faster.

"Heath!" she pleaded, the hairs on the back of her neck rising.

When his voice still didn't answer her call, she swallowed deeply as she realized what this could only mean. Heath wasn't in Heaven, and he was too good to have gone to the Hollow, or Hell as others outside her village called it—that meant he was confined somewhere in the ghost realm … with the Headless Horseman.

A ghost only moved on once they resolved their unfinished business. No one but a seer could witness the ghosts around them, but even if Beatrice knew one, it wouldn't matter since a ghost was unable to converse with them. Unless they were a seer too, which she knew Heath was not.

Beatrice collected her thoughts and settled on what would have to be done. "It's the only way, Heath," she whispered, then bounded toward her home.

Her brother was no longer in the sitting room when she entered their pristine manor, and her mother would still be locked away in the library. She and her mother had always been distant from one another, most likely because Beatrice had been an unwelcomed accident.

Taking a black dress from her wardrobe, she spruced herself up for the evening ball. She powdered her face and eyelids, then added a stroke of blush to her cheeks and dark rouge to accentuate her lips. After penning a letter to her family and resting it on her pillow, she placed a dark ribbon necklace around her throat, an obsidian stone hanging at its center. The mirror reflected her unkempt red hair, and she pinned her curled locks up until she looked presentable. Rather than being a wallflower for the night as she would've proudly done, Beatrice planned to meet a certain rogue who she hoped would be in attendance.

With one last look at her image in the mirror, she went down to the sitting room, where Claude waited in a high-backed velvet chair. He wore fine attire while sipping from a silver flask.

Beatrice rolled her eyes. "You could've at least waited until we arrived at the ball to start drinking."

He angled his head in her direction and arched a brow as he observed her. "What are you planning?"

"Whatever do you mean?" She smiled brightly while slipping on her lacy gloves.

Claude tucked away the flask and adjusted his cravat. "You're on time, I didn't have to call on you once, you're not bickering about attending, and you're dressed to impress."

Beatrice shrugged. "Be happy then."

"I suppose you truly don't want to join a nunnery," he grunted before leading her outside to the carriage. They remained silent all the way to the town manor.

Claude grasped Beatrice's hand and helped her down from the carriage. The manor was one of the largest in their village and owned by the head witch of the council.

Candlelight shone through the tall windows, and the moon illuminated the tulip gardens and the many statues. A few lone bats perched on the roof of the manor, staring down at those who approached the home.

A piano and violins played, their music growing louder as Beatrice and Claude entered the manor. Along the walls, tiny plants hung, their leaves like arms swaying to the melody. Bringing plants to life was something Beatrice was envious she couldn't achieve.

The hall opened to an extravagant ballroom, obsidian chandeliers dangling from the ceiling. The crowd of guests sipped from their wine glasses while others gossiped and danced.

Her brother's attention caught on a woman whose cleavage was perfectly propped up. When her eyes met his, she flashed him a flirtatious smile.

This was the perfect opportunity for Beatrice to be alone. "Go talk to her. I'll be fine," she encouraged.

Claude studied Beatrice, his eyes narrowing. "Don't wander off."

She crossed her fingers behind her back and lied, "Of course not."

Once her brother and his lover disappeared down a dim hallway, Beatrice surveyed the room, her gaze drifting from face to face. A warlock attempted to woo a young dark-haired woman while juggling balls in the air without using his hands.

Beatrice snorted and continued searching through the sea of people until she found the man she'd been wishing for. He faced the opposite direction, his long, sleek black hair hanging past his shoulders. Black velvet attire covered Rainier's lithe build from head to toe. One of his pale hands was against the wall as he chatted with a beautiful blonde woman.

Taking a steady breath, Beatrice skirted around dancing couples to reach him.

"Excuse me, sir." She tapped Rainier on his shoulder, and he slowly turned around.

"Yes?" he purred, his purple irises sweeping over her. "Aren't you the little dark flower tonight."

The woman he'd been pursuing tightened her expression, clearly unhappy that Beatrice had interrupted the pair. Rainier was a vampire, known to dabble in pleasure time and time again yet never fall in love.

"Let's go somewhere quiet," Beatrice said, her pulse anxious to begin.

"You're rather forward," he cooed while trailing an elegant digit across his shapely lower lip.

"Neither of us will regret it." Beatrice grasped his hand, and he didn't resist when she led him out into the cool night behind the manor.

As she faced him, his hand cupped her cheek and he whispered in her ear, "If it's pleasure you seek, know that it's all I will provide. Nothing else."

"There will be no pleasure of that kind tonight," Beatrice answered, stepping back from his touch.

Rainier blinked as though he'd never once been refused. "And what is it you want then, dark flower?"

"Drink my blood. All of it." Her tone came out assured.

"Ah, I see." He chuckled. "If you want to end

your life, you don't need my assistance."

"I *do*. I must end up a ghost to help someone I care dearly about."

"Caring too much is a fault." He paused, his lavender gaze blazing. "But if this is what you wish, then I won't deny you."

Beatrice nodded, confident of her decision. "No pleasure though. Even if I beg for it."

His smile grew wolfish. "Now that is something you might regret, dark flower."

Ignoring his taunt, she tilted her head to give the vampire access to her flesh. Rainier's sharp fangs dropped, and his teeth grazed the crook of her neck before piercing her flesh.

Beatrice gasped, her eyelids fluttering at the sharp pain taking root. Only, it didn't last long—the affliction morphed into something ravenous. A new hunger stirred within her as the vampire drank, her hands roaming down the front of his chest, to the button of his trousers. Rainier captured her wrists and continued to feast on her while she pleaded with him to give her pleasure.

The lustful feeling changed to something else, lighter, freer, as though she were falling from the starry, night sky.

Beatrice shut her eyes when exhaustion poured over her, draining her from the inside out. And then, as if she hadn't been tired at all, she flicked open her lids after she no longer felt Rainier's fangs.

The vampire had vanished.

She peered down at herself and realized she was, in fact, the one who'd left him. Her form was a translucent soft ivory glow—her skin, her dress, her shoes. *Everything.*

Beatrice's wish had come true.

She was a ghost.

No heartbeat. No need to breathe. Beatrice was now a member of the deceased. With a relieved smile that her soul hadn't passed on to Heaven or the Hollow, she flexed an alabaster hand before her. Allowing Rainier to drain her of life had been risky—it could've gone terribly wrong, but she'd clung on to the fact that she would have unfinished business.

Heath.

Her dear friend had to be somewhere in this realm. She observed her surroundings and found herself still at the manor, where not a single ghost lingered inside when she peered through the parted curtains of a window.

As she drew back, an ivory, translucent woman, *ghost*, rounded the manor. The stranger's pearlescent hair hung in matted waves down to her waist, her gown torn and frayed.

"Hello!" Beatrice called and met up with the woman. The ghost didn't halt her movements even when Beatrice tapped her on the shoulder. She kept up with the ghost's quickened pace and asked, "Have you seen a man named Heath?"

The ghost stilled, slowly turning to face Beatrice. "He's Heath," the woman moaned, pointing toward a sycamore tree, then she pivoted and knelt beside a bush. "And so is he, and him, and oh, most certainly him." The ghost clasped her hands as she smiled widely, her face full of pride.

Beatrice's lips formed a tight line, and she didn't dare follow the woman any longer into her mad world. She was certainly not well, a ghost trapped inside her own mind. What if Heath was facing the same precise circumstance? Even if he was, she would find a way to snap him out of that state. It didn't matter if she had to wait seasons upon seasons for him to answer her.

Perhaps Heath's ghost resided inside the small cottage on her property where he'd died. If he wasn't there, she would continue hunting him down through the village until she discovered him, regardless if the Headless Horseman was lurking about.

As she passed several shops, a shrill voice shouted, "Beatrice!"

She halted in her tracks and wandered toward an older woman wearing a simple dress with large buttons lining the front.

"Mrs. Wallace?" Beatrice blinked, studying the pale villager who'd recently died in her florist shop.

"I thought that was you," the woman said, placing a hand on Beatrice's shoulder. "It's a pity you're here."

Beatrice shrugged. "Don't feel sorry for me. I'm searching for Heath. Would you happen to have seen him?" At least once a week, her mother used to send Heath or Beatrice to pick up special flowers from Mrs. Wallace's shop.

The woman shook her head. "No, I'm sorry, but I haven't."

"If you see Heath, tell him I'm here searching for him." Beatrice took off running once more, and as she approached the cemetery, she slowed her steps.

Apparitions lingered around several of the headstones, but none of them were Heath. She walked through the dew-covered grass toward his grave, yet it was empty of any dead. No Headless Horseman in sight either. Perhaps her village was mistaken, and the vengeful ghost truly was nothing but a myth.

Further behind her, a gorgeous young woman

with elegant curves and a small waist spun in circles while shouting something Beatrice couldn't make out. A name possibly?

There were too many people here with their own unsolved issues for Beatrice to fret over, so she left the cemetery and hurried toward her family's property. The light from the crescent moon and the twinkling stars guided her way down the trail, and just as she cut through the woods near her parents' manor, bushes rustled behind her. Heavy footsteps pounded against the earth, and she whirled around to find a tall, translucent, ivory beast hovering above her.

Twisted antlers protruded from a deer skull, the beast's furred limbs too long and gangly to match his body. Sharp claws extended out of the creature's gnarled fingers, and his shoulders hunched, his head leaning forward at an unnatural angle. He stood on his hind legs, his sunken chest displaying ribs that appeared as if they would tear through his skin at any moment.

"Where is Heath?" Beatrice growled, tightening her fists and taking a measured step backward.

"Bea?" Bewilderment filled his voice.

She stared into the glowing white orbs of the beast's eye sockets, attempting to decipher any lies or trickery, though the creature could never speak before when he took over Heath's body and mind. "You're *you*?" she finally exclaimed. "Not the wendigo?"

"It's me. I vow it," he said.

"Prove it first." She watched as his tail swayed behind him like a pendulum.

"Simple. You sometimes purchase spells from witches to have your parents believe you're better than you are."

"Heath!" Beatrice beamed, unable to hold back her excitement. She threw herself forward and wrapped her arms around his crooked frame. Never had she been this close to his other form, to where she could feel his bones. "How are you the wendigo?"

Heath returned the embrace, bringing her closer. "I've been trapped in this murderer's form ever since the wendigo ripped my heart out, unfortunately. It's been … an adjustment." He shifted back and grasped her upper arms with his large hands. "What happened to you? You should be at home."

"Isn't it clear enough? I'm dead."

"Did someone hurt you?" he ground out.

"Not in the way you're imagining." She lifted her chin in defiance, knowing he wouldn't approve of the next aspect. "However, I did ask a vampire to drink all of my blood."

"A vampire?" Heath hissed. "Whyever would you do something so ridiculous? Please tell me it wasn't *Rainier*."

"It was Rainier," she said nonchalantly.

Heath released a string of curses. "That scoundrel? Did he take advantage of you?"

"He wasn't untoward. I told him I didn't want pleasure, and he made certain it didn't occur. Even with me not acting myself." And why was she explaining this to him instead of just answering no? Heath wasn't courting her... "None of that matters anyhow. It took far too long for Jeanne to finally give me a brew to contact the dead. I had to give you a proper goodbye, but when you didn't answer my call, I knew you were trapped here." Beatrice held back a sob, realizing that saying goodbye would not have been enough for her to move on.

"So you ended your life for *me*?" His deep baritone rose an octave.

"Oh, hush!" she chided. "There's no altering the past." Her family wouldn't grieve for long, if at all, once they discovered the letter in her room explaining why she'd chosen to leave.

Heath released a low, animalistic sound. "What if you pass on before I do and I'm still trapped here? Then there would've been no purpose of sacrificing yourself."

Beatrice had considered that, amongst other things. "I believe that's highly unlikely since my unfinished business is to help you. And if I were to wager what yours is, it's to get you out of this blasted wendigo form."

"No witch could find a solution before, and this

is much different," he said, his voice resigned.

"Then you underestimate my determination. I might be quite the calamity when it comes to spells, but that doesn't mean I won't rid you of this bastard beast."

"So, I heard your father mention to Claude that you'll be attending the upcoming ball," Heath said as he ripped a beet from the ground. Dirt smeared the front of his white shirt, and sweat dotted his brow and slicked his curly blond hair.

"Oh, that." Beatrice grinned while walking across the wooden beam of the raised herb garden. "I'm an overripened apple that appears to not have enough time left to find a husband. They must believe I'll be withered and gray by this time next year."

"Nonsense, you could always spell yourself to remain youthful if you chose, but I prefer to see each line and wrinkle you earn." Heath winked. He tossed another beet into the wheelbarrow. "I take it you are going then?"

Beatrice would rather not, but at least it would get her father and brother off her back for a little while. "I am, but between you and me"—she lowered her voice—"I'm planning to remain a wallflower at the ball. You're welcome to attend and keep me company. I knight you as my guard to ward off any unwanted attention since we both know my brother will be busy tumbling someone."

Heath's dusky brown eyes met hers, and he gave Beatrice a lopsided grin. "For your protection, I'll be there."

She performed a pirouette on the beam, wobbling and almost losing her balance. "As long as you promise not to dance with a certain werewolf named Cathy, then the night will be grand." Something about Cathy dancing in the company of Heath made Beatrice's blood boil, and particularly when she imagined them off in a shadowy corner, his hand gliding slowly up Cathy's thigh. Unreasonable, she knew. But the werewolf was a shrew who delighted in courting men, only to easily toss them aside for someone shiny and new.

He arched a brow. "I don't fancy Cathy."

Beatrice's smile spread, grateful. "She believes you two are destined since you could be the Heathcliff to her Cathy. Wuthering Heights reincarnate yet having a more pleasant ending."

"How quaint," he drawled with zero enthusiasm.

Beatrice snickered. As she completed another appalling pirouette in the opposite direction, she stumbled, falling sideways, and knocked Heath to the ground.

"I was so close to perfecting that," she lied.

Heath wrapped an arm around her and sat up with her

still in his lap. "Clumsy little thing, aren't you?" He chuckled, his laughter deep and comforting.

Her pulse sped at Heath's nearness, at his amber scent, but she told herself it was only because she'd never been in a man's lap before.

Beneath the sun, she could've sworn Heath's pupils were dilated as he said, "Perhaps at the ball, you and—" His words cut off, and the color drained from his face. "I need to get inside my cage. Now!"

She leapt from Heath's lap, then they fled toward his cottage. He tore open the door, and they hurried into his bedroom where the iron cage rested near his desk.

"You don't need to be here for this," he said while crouching inside, his fingers fidgeting.

Beatrice shut the cage door and locked it for him. "What better things are there for me to do today? I can think of none," she jested, attempting to lighten the mood.

Heath opened his mouth to speak but instead gripped his chest and released a guttural, irritable growl. The browns of his irises swallowed up his eyes and turned pitch-black as they rolled backward. His bones cracked and snapped, the harsh sounds reverberating throughout the room.

Beatrice swallowed deeply when his body writhed as though he were possessed by a vicious demon of the Hollow. She'd watched this torture happen once a season over the years, but she always knew it was only temporary and that he would return to himself the following day.

Heath bellowed savagely, his teeth sharpening, his veins bulging from his flesh. The clothing he wore ripped, his face elongated, paling and hardening before turning into a deer skull. Dark fur sprouted from his skin, a long, thin tail breaking free behind him. Claws pierced from his fingertips, his body folding forward, hunching, both crooked and menacing.

The wendigo's obsidian gaze locked on hers, and he slammed his body against the cage door while letting out a devilish shriek.

Beatrice glowered at the creature. "Can't you just let him be?"

No one in the village had found a cure for Heath, not even the most powerful witch—the Crowned Witch. Heath's mother had been with child when a wendigo slipped inside the strong witch's body. Heath's father killed his mother after she attempted to eat her newborn infant. A part of the wendigo had slithered inside Heath during his mother's pregnancy, yet he'd been lucky that he was free from the creature for most of the year.

"One day, Heath will rid himself of you," Beatrice said between gritted teeth.

The wendigo hissed at her, and its expression morphed into something chilling. Something insidious. He appeared to be smiling at her, all while lifting his hand, then driving his claws into his chest as though in retaliation against her words.

Beatrice screamed and unlocked the cage, but it was too late. Like a prize, the beast held up Heath's bloody heart before collapsing to his death.

Heath's death.

"Has the wendigo's *wonderful* personality come out, or has he remained tamed and at bay?" Beatrice asked, keeping her voice steady even though she trembled at the memory of the beast clutching Heath's heart.

"He has." Heath sighed. "Being trapped in this state makes things unpredictable."

"That bastard," Beatrice ground out, then folded her arms around him once more, tears brimming her eyes. "I'm sorry I couldn't do more for you that day. I didn't know he would—"

"There was nothing you could've done, Bea." He drew back and tilted her chin so their gazes met. "On the bright side, I haven't eaten anyone."

"That's good news," she said, relieved. A wendigo was much different than a werewolf—once the foul creature tasted human flesh, the body it clung to truly belonged to the beast, and no one could escape its demands then. If Heath had remained a ravenous beast, the council would've gotten involved and ended his life to protect the village from such an unstable creature.

Thunderous horse hooves pounded against the earth, coming in their direction. Beatrice jolted, and Heath grasped her by the arms, then drew her to his chest behind a large tree trunk.

Even in his ghostly state, Heath felt just as firm against her as the day when she'd fallen on top of him and he'd held her. "It's not who I think it is, is it?" she finally said.

"It is," he whispered in her ear.

Beatrice peered out from the tree, and her eyes widened when she caught sight of a powerful pale stallion carrying a rider. The man's long cape cracked against the wind, his head nowhere to be found. *The Headless Horseman.* She could now confirm that he was no myth at all.

Once the horse and the headless ghost faded into the distance, Beatrice turned to face Heath, his arm still draped around her waist. "Does he ride all day?" she murmured.

"Only at night. And not once has he ever missed coming out after dark since I've been here."

Throughout the rest of the night, Beatrice and Heath remained in the cellar of her home—away from the Headless Horseman—where she worked on uncovering a solution for her friend's unfortunate condition. Failures. All of them. No tincture reversed his current wendigo state. The only individual ingredients she couldn't touch were human or animal remains. No bones. No teeth. No hair. No organs. If she needed to create a whole new brew by using them, it wouldn't be possible, and she would just have to try substituting the ingredients with something else.

All was quiet in the house above them, and

Beatrice wondered if her parents had learned of her death yet, had read the letter she'd left for them. Rainier wouldn't be at fault either—the village knew that if one asked a vampire to drink their blood, the immortal most certainly would, and if one wanted the vampire to drink them dry, the request would not be denied.

Not a single ounce of exhaustion swept over Beatrice after her demise, and she was content by that fact since she could work on remedies to break Heath's miserable plight. She wouldn't give up until he was released from the wendigo so they could both pass on together.

"There's nothing in this one either." The sound of Heath shutting the tome echoed off the walls.

"We'll find something, and when you move on, I move on," Beatrice said with a small smile over her shoulder as she watched Heath pore over another spell book.

"And if you stay, I stay." He bared his teeth in a wide grin. For the first time, she found the wendigo rather adorable, but only because the creature was Heath.

"Drink this." Beatrice handed Heath a small vial. He'd already tried several, but the outcome had been the same—no change.

Heath took the brew from her, his clawed fingers gently brushing hers, and even though coldness enveloped her as a ghost, warmth briefly filled her for those meager moments until his digits left her.

She studied him while he tilted back the vial and drank, and she waited impatiently.

No reversal.

Again.

Beatrice released a frustrated, unintelligible sound. "That's the last one I have that might've worked." It was a potion she'd bought from a witch that generally reversed a spell when Beatrice made a mistake. But Heath wasn't truly under a spell … this was something different. "We could slip into one of the witches' cellars and see if I can find something else to try." That was if their homes weren't warded against ghosts. Most were, especially the powerful witches and warlocks who wanted to keep the creation of their spells a secret.

"We'll try," Heath agreed.

Before they left, Beatrice collected a handbag and tucked a few tinctures inside in case they came across anything dangerous. The Headless Horseman being at the top of that list.

They left the cellar and trekked through the village, passing an array of other ghosts, most staring at Heath with saucered eyes, clearly believing he might attack them at any given moment. Each of the witch or warlock homes they tried to enter were protected against ghosts, just as she'd suspected, and Beatrice wasn't knowledgeable enough to break their spells. They easily entered a couple of cottages, only there was nothing of importance that she hadn't already had in her own cellar—not on the shelves, nor in the cupboards or drawers. The wards were even stronger at the council manor, and she kicked the door, cursing it in frustration.

Near the edge of the village stood an alluring black manor without any windows shining beneath the sun's rays, its ornate turrets glistening.

Rainier's home.

"He isn't a warlock, but perhaps we can find something of use in there since he's been around for centuries," Beatrice suggested.

Heath folded his arms over his chest once they reached the vampire's doorstep.

"Are you still angry with him?"

"For sinking his fangs into you? Of course I am."

Beatrice rolled her eyes and stepped over the threshold. An elegant onyx staircase rested before her in a large circular sitting room where dark velvet settees and chairs lingered on top of black-furred rugs. Portraits of naked women in elegant positions hung across the walls in silver frames.

"His home is just as I expected," Heath said, peering up at a painting of a woman with her back arched, her face angelic, as she held a cherry over her parted lips.

Approaching footsteps sounded along the stairs, and Beatrice glanced up them to find a female carrying a lantern, a long nightgown brushing her ankles. The ghost's hair was in disarray, her curls flowing down her back.

"Hello," Beatrice called, but the ghost ignored her, reaching the last step, then wandering right back up them.

"You see what happens to Rainier's lovers?" Heath pointed out.

"It's not his fault they have unfinished business." She tugged his arm to follow her down the hall, thankful that neither he nor she were in that sort of wretched state.

They searched every room on the first floor, finding only a collection of coffins and mundane things.

Heath followed Beatrice up the staircase, and they came to a library with shelves standing from floor to ceiling. Six female ghosts were in the room, two in chairs, one reading a book on a chaise, and the others lying on a furred rug.

All six of them peered toward Beatrice and Heath with wide eyes. "Don't mind him—he won't attack," Beatrice assured them. "Would any of you happen to be witches?"

The woman on the chaise sat up and placed her book beside her. She wore a silk gown, the swells of her breasts spilling above her lacy neckline. "I'm a witch," she said, her gaze fastened on Heath as if she believed Beatrice had been lying about him.

Beatrice stepped in front of Heath to veer the

witch's attention to her. "He used to only become a wendigo once each season. But ever since he died in this state, he's remained this way. Do you think you could help him?"

The woman gracefully pushed up from the chaise, and Beatrice moved aside to allow the witch to properly inspect Heath. She placed a hand against his sternum, closed her eyes, and softly chanted.

Lifting her palm from Heath after about a minute passed, she observed him. "You need time."

Heath nodded as Beatrice asked, "Time for what?"

"Just time." The witch shrugged. "No brews. No new spells. He'll either turn back, or he won't. That is up to you, and that is all I will say."

Beatrice scowled. "You're being vague. I know when a witch doesn't want to speak the truth."

Heath clasped her hand. "She spoke enough."

"I suppose," she muttered, not wanting to uncover how powerful the witch could be if they angered her. A curse upon them would only make matters worse.

There wasn't a need to search Rainier's home any further, and Beatrice's curiosity wasn't interested to see what surprises could be in the other rooms. Even when they went back into the afternoon sunlight, she continued to frown. *The witch probably relishes the fret she causes with her partial truths.*

Heath gently grasped Beatrice's arm, and she

turned to face him. His glowing eyes held hers as he cradled her face. "No grudges. I know how you get. Focus on you and me. No one else."

"Fine," she relented and wrapped her arms around him, resting her head against his chest. "I just want to resolve this for you."

"You haven't been here a full day. Relax," Heath said, his hand gently stroking her back. "My issue doesn't have to be yours."

Beatrice stared up at him, unblinking. "*Relax*? You're still in wendigo form, and the beast could slip out at any moment."

"I'll warn you as I always do," he promised.

She nodded with a long exhale and walked beside Heath.

They left Rainier's gardens, then ventured down through the market, unsure of what to do next. Should they simply wait and hope time alone would truly cure Heath?

As they passed the florist shop, two strong hands clamped down on Beatrice's shoulders and shook her like a toy rattle. She spun out from the stranger's grip to find the Headless Horseman behind her. Releasing a high-pitched scream, she kicked the ghost in the stomach.

Heath pulled her backward before she could strike him again. "Stop," he said, "that isn't the Headless Horseman."

Beatrice stilled, inspecting the ghost from neck

to toe, realizing that, indeed, Heath was correct in his assessment.

"A victim." She heaved a sigh. "I'm sorry, sir." But she was unsure if the ghost could even hear or see her. Either way, the man didn't approach her, only stood there, seeming to wait for something. "What do you think he needs?" she asked Heath.

He ran a clawed hand against the side of his skull. "His head perhaps?"

Beatrice mulled this over. "If he wasn't one of the Headless Horseman's victims in this realm, and he originally died from decapitation, then possibly." She surveyed the man further, noticing a woman's locket around his neck. Slowly stepping forward, as to not frighten the ghost, she opened the locket, and her lips parted at the recognizable pictures inside.

"It's Mr. Maddock!" she announced. The old baker's wife died ten years ago, and every day after that he'd continued to mourn for her, yet not once had he ever visited her grave. "I believe I know what his unfinished business is. Since we have *time* as the witch said, we could take him to the cemetery."

"It's the right thing to do," Heath agreed.

On either side of Mr. Maddock, they guided him up the road to the cemetery. Mr. Maddock didn't resist them even a fraction, seeming to know where he was being led. Or perhaps hoping.

They helped him kneel before his wife's grave marker, stone angels carved atop it. Beatrice grasped

Mr. Maddock's hand and pressed his palm to his wife's name on the headstone.

"You're here now," Beatrice said softly. "Your wife will be waiting for you." It wasn't something she knew for certain, but she had to trust her gut.

If Mr. Maddock didn't pass on, then there was nothing else she could do for him.

As Beatrice and Heath watched though, Mr. Maddock's ivory form grew paler, more translucent, his essence fading away until he was no longer waiting to leave this place.

He was gone.

Heath shifted closer and tucked a loose lock of hair behind her ear. "You did good, Bea."

His blazing gaze stayed trained on her, and she huffed, "What? Is there something on my face?"

"You look very angelic in this form is all." His jaw lowered, making his teeth widen into a smile.

Beatrice cupped the side of his skull. "Hmm… And how did I look before? Damnable?" she drawled.

"Never," he rasped.

"Well, Heath, you appear positively charming."

He chuckled. "Not beastly?"

"Perhaps slightly." She laughed softly. "Nevertheless, you're *you*." Heath stiffened under her touch, and she dropped her arm by her side. "What is it?"

"Don't follow me. You need to run," he said

gruffly, then bolted away from the cemetery and into the woods.

She knew at once the wendigo was trying to take over and she wouldn't run from him, not when there was a possibility for Heath to remain gone. Clutching her skirts, she darted after him and wove around the trees until she found him hunched near a rotting trunk.

"I told you to run," he groaned, gripping the side of his skull.

"I did as you asked, but toward you instead. Not away. *Never* away."

"Stubborn woman. You have to go," he growled, his body jerking, his clawed fingers twitching.

"Trust me, I know what I'm doing." Even if they were back in the world of the living, her heart wouldn't have beat with fear, only clenched onto the determination to give him safety and freedom from this beast.

"But I'm not entirely foolish either," Beatrice added when the familiar writhing of the wendigo stirred. She scurried up a nearby tree and peered down at Heath from a thick branch.

Fingers digging into the bark, Beatrice released a loud whistle. The wendigo snapped his wicked gaze to hers, and a deep, starved growl barreled out from him. He shot forward and clawed at the tree trunk, his razor-sharp teeth glinting, begging for a taste of her. One fact she knew about wendigos was that they couldn't climb things the way a werewolf could.

"Come here, pretty beastie," she sang while opening her handbag tied at her waist. "Do you want to take a bite of my flesh? I warn you, I might be bitter."

The wendigo snarled and rattled the branch just below her. She drew out a spelled stone and tightened her fist around it. As he prowled beneath her, she hurled the stone at his skull.

The creature screeched, his head thrown back toward the sky while he convulsed, his knees buckling. He collapsed to the ground at an awkward angle, and his body quaked for a few more moments before stilling.

"Heath?" Beatrice called, her eyes widening at his motionless form. Jeanne had taught her how to make the stones and told her a lady should always carry a couple in case danger lurked about. The stones were light, but when the owner threw one, the blow would feel more weighted, strike harder.

Her brow furrowed as she peered down at the creature—a wendigo wasn't smart enough to pretend as though he were unconscious. However, he could still awaken. Grasping another spelled stone, she climbed down the tree. A sudden fear churned within her—what if she'd hurt Heath and he never awoke?

Beatrice held the stone higher, her hand trembling. "Heath, are you in there?"

"I feel as if I've been struck by a stone," he groaned, his head lolling to the side.

With a reassured sigh, Beatrice knelt beside him and entwined her fingers with his. "I'm so sorry. It was the only thing I had that could stop the bastard."

He stayed silent, his glowing orbs still unlit in their sockets. And then something tickled her palm, and she gasped at what rested before her. Heath's fur and claws slipped inside his skin, revealing a human hand, though still ghostly pale. His arms did the same, becoming furless once more.

"You're curing!" Beatrice exclaimed.

She craned her neck and watched as the lower half of his skull faded and altered into something else entirely. Heath's familiar, strong jaw, accompanied by his shapely lips. Yet the top portion of the wendigo's skull didn't vanish. It looked as though a mask were covering most of his face.

Perhaps she could remove it… Beatrice brushed a finger across the snout and attempted to lift it, but the skull remained planted. "I was wrong. You're cured only a smidge."

This was something entirely new—never had there been a time where he'd been in a partial wendigo-human state besides during shifting.

The white orbs lit up as he finally opened his eyes, his gaze not wavering from hers. "You're doing it," he whispered.

"I haven't done anything except nearly split your

skull into two," she huffed.

"Ah, but you didn't, Bea."

Beatrice and Heath stayed in the woods until the stars dotted the sky's inky darkness, the new moon hidden from prying eyes. Every so often, she snuck glances in his direction. Not once was there ever an instance where she'd been privy to seeing his exposed upper arms before. Muscular and manly and… An unexpected heat pooled low in her belly and she blinked, then focused back on the night sky, hoping he hadn't witnessed her untoward behavior.

"You've been quiet a long while," Heath said, his bare arm so very near to brushing hers. "It's unlike you."

A grin spread her cheeks. "Do you miss the

sound of my voice already?"

"Always." He lifted his arm in invitation for her to chat with him in the way she always had in the past. She'd never hesitated about curling up beside him. Her friend. And more than ever before she wanted to lean in, drape her arms around his waist, but what was different now? Why was she being quiet?

"The wendigo is gone," he promised.

Beatrice finally rested her head in the crook of his arm. Even though his essence was cool against her, his embrace sent a blissful lick of warmth through her. Her eyelids fluttered as she held Heath tightly. She'd missed him for the past two weeks was all, but the more they lingered in the quiet, the more she wanted to trail a finger across his lips.

"Do you remember the night I snuck out my window?" she asked in an attempt to distract herself.

"Which time?" And she heard the mischievous smile in his voice.

"The night I took a bottle of wine from my parents' collection and we got drunk off it for the first time." Beatrice remembered impatiently waiting for her mother to leave the library and go to sleep, so she could retrieve one from a spot that her parents would never notice.

"You're such a *terrible* influence," Heath drawled, his thumb rubbing her arm and sending a delicious shiver up her spine.

Her parents were absolutely furious when she'd returned the following morning in a rumpled state. It was believed she'd tumbled Heath, and her father had threatened to send her to the nunnery. "My father was horrid to you before he used one of Jeanne's truth spells on us." After it revealed Beatrice had been mostly at fault, she'd received the brunt of the punishment.

"I deserved his harsh words," Heath said.

She peered up at him and frowned. "Why would you deserve him calling you such things?"

The glow of his eyes brightened. "That night, I was tempted to kiss you… To do ungentlemanly things with you."

If Beatrice had breath, it would've hitched. "*Oh.*" She bit her lip as she thought about that unforgettable night, how she hadn't wanted to be anywhere else but with Heath. Yet she hadn't realized it then, not until at that precise moment. She was *fancying* him, and she knew with her entire being if he'd kissed her that night, she would've realized it sooner.

While collecting her courage to tell him how she felt, a loud screech tore through the air, making her jolt. They leapt to their feet and rushed further into the woods toward the frantic sounds.

"You rutting bastard!" a woman screeched. "I'm not a fragile daisy. Make it *harder*!"

Beatrice skirted around a tree and halted beside

Heath, her mouth agape. A voluptuous woman rested on all fours while a husky man thrust into her from behind, their clothing scattered around the woods, their moans harsh. The two ghosts fixed their narrowed gazes on Beatrice and Heath, not once breaking from their activity, their bodies smacking as one. Beatrice had never witnessed such intense, angry pleasure. Or anyone in a lustful act for that matter. She'd only ever imagined how it could feel.

"Do you mind?" the man growled over his shoulder at them.

"Or do you prefer to join us?" the woman moaned.

"No, but thank you," Beatrice said as a burst of laughter bubbled up her throat. She grabbed Heath's hand and pulled him through the woods toward the trail leading to her home. "That was quite entertaining."

"Mmm," he said gruffly.

"Were you tempted to join her?" Beatrice asked when curiosity and something akin to envy stirred within her.

His gaze trained on hers, unyielding. "Not with her."

Beatrice swore on her life as a witch that her nonexistent heart fluttered at his words. She opened her mouth to ask him, *then who*, when, for once, she found herself too shy to ask. What if he did admit it was her? But what if he didn't? "Perhaps we should return to the cemetery," she said instead. "I could cast a spell over your grave. There isn't a way for me to physically touch your corpse, but it could potentially speed up time." If it would help keep the wendigo at bay, she needed to at least attempt it.

"I'll accompany you there then." He held out his arm for her when a horse's hooves pummeled the earth, its already familiar boisterous noises surrounding them.

Beatrice's stomach sank, but before she could think which way to go, Heath grasped her arm and whisper-shouted, "This way, Bea."

As they fled toward the cemetery, the horse and its rider broke out from the woods just behind them. The Headless Horseman cradled a glowing orange jack-o'-lantern in one arm, the stallion's hoofbeats approaching.

Heath yanked her between two trees, and she glanced back toward the ghost. The Headless Horseman's upper torso turned in their direction, but he didn't reach for his sword, nor did he follow them.

She tugged on Heath and they stopped running, watching as the ghost disappeared from their sight.

"I suppose our heads aren't up to par for him," Beatrice jested, though she still worried he could return. She assumed he collected others' heads as revenge for his inability to find his own.

"He's a fool without taste then," Heath grunted.

"Certainly true." Beatrice smiled. She peered down and gasped, stumbling backward. "You're practically bare!" His legs and feet were no longer covered in fur, their human shape returned.

Heath cocked his head as he inspected himself. "And so I am."

Beatrice's gaze veered from his sunken chest to between his legs, where his manhood was hidden. If that part of him was revealed next, she knew it would be perfect, just like all the rest of Heath.

She cleared her throat, realizing *what* she was focused on. "The witch was accurate—all you need is time." Perhaps Beatrice coming into the ghost realm hadn't mattered at all. She'd wanted to be the one to save him, to prove that she could do something right as a witch and help the person she cared most about.

"Do you regret asking Rainier to end your life?" Heath asked, his voice soft.

"Not in all the centuries combined." Beatrice knew why she'd come to him so easily, why as soon as she discovered he wasn't in the afterlife, she didn't hesitate to make certain she became a ghost.

She didn't only fancy Heath—she was in love with him.

As Beatrice and Heath trekked toward the cemetery, she kept an eye out for the Headless Horseman in case he rode back in their direction. But the murderous ghost wasn't what she was most concerned about at the moment.

How could she have been so foolish and not known she was *in love* with her dearest friend? She saw now that this was why she'd avoided attending any ball, had refused her parents' advice when they'd told her what qualities she should search for in a husband.

Heath must've returned her affections if he'd wanted to kiss her once. Or had it only been the wine influencing him?

Together, they entered the cemetery, where a light fog had rolled in over the grass. The residing ghosts didn't approach but studied Heath's partial-wendigo form with wary gazes. She led him to his grave, and his fingers brushed the crafted wooden cross she'd made and the withered flowers atop the dirt. After he was buried, she'd brought him daffodils from her garden each day.

He gently lifted her chin between his thumb and forefinger, then murmured, "Thank you for the flowers and the grave marker."

"You don't know if those were from me." She smiled.

"I do." Beneath the shadows of his skull, she could see his impeccable grin. His *very* kissable lips.

"Fine, it was me," she said slowly, kneeling in front of his grave while watching him from the corners of her eyes. Opening her handbag, she fished out a small vial and sprinkled the blue-tinted brew over his burial site.

Beatrice closed her eyes, then pressed her hands to the soft dirt, attempting to locate his decaying corpse. Only a handful of seconds passed when it struck her in the chest. *There.* She could feel the dead heart that had been tucked back inside the corpse's chest, his rotting flesh, his bones. And something else. His body was partially wendigo just as Heath was now. But besides that, there was nothing to reel toward them and place inside Heath to progress time.

It was truly up to fate.

As she brushed her hands against the skirts of her dress and stood, a quartet of violins played a cheerful melody at the edge of the cemetery. Three couples found one another and danced to the music as though they were at a fancy ball.

"Care to dance?" Heath asked, holding his hand out toward her.

Of course she would—he was the only man she'd want to dance with. "This means I'm not a wallflower," she teased and placed her dainty hand in his.

"Never."

"First, let me give you something." Beatrice skimmed her fingertips up his bare arm and spoke a low incantation. She smiled as a pale coat, shirt, cravat, trousers, and boots cloaked his muscular form. "There. A prim and proper partial wendigo."

Heath chuckled and dipped his head toward hers. "So, you could've given me trousers all along?"

"I do have a couple of tricks up my sleeve." She laughed.

The violinists continued to play their song as Heath led Beatrice to the middle of the cemetery. He drew her to his chest, his palm dipping to her lower back, and they danced in circles around the headstones. She bit her lip, yearning for this moment to never end.

They danced and danced through another two songs until the quartet fell silent. Beatrice lay her head against his shoulder, not wanting to break apart just yet, so they continued their movements to the melancholic song of the wind.

After a long while of swaying in the fog, she lifted her hand to the side of Heath's skull, wishing she could touch his cheek instead.

"I love you," she murmured. "I should've realized this a long time ago." It was an important piece that she could no longer keep to herself.

And then, before her very eyes, she watched as he transformed, the wendigo's skull fading, replaced by the face she knew so well. Even though his hair and eye color were the same shade as any other ghost, to her, his were the most beautiful.

Heath was himself again, and yet, he remained in the cemetery. Beatrice furrowed her brow. "You're you again, but you haven't moved on."

"No, I haven't," he whispered and brushed a loose tendril of hair behind her ear. "When I first arrived here, I came across a ghost and recognized her as my mother. I knew her features well from my father's favorite portrait of her. When speaking to her, I discovered she'd placed a spell on me before her death, one where I needed to hear the words of true love to break what I've always considered a curse. That was my mother's unfinished business, to give me the message before she passed on."

Beatrice covered her mouth with a gasp. "Why didn't you tell me sooner? I could've confessed my love at once!"

"I would've never burdened you with such a thing," he said. "It didn't matter if I had to spend eternity as a wendigo, I wouldn't have forced you to say you loved me if you did not."

"But I do." Beatrice's eyes widened, and her hands trembled. "I meant what I said!"

"There's a second part—it was for me to say the words in return." Heath paused, gently caressing her face. "I've loved you forever, Beatrice Walker. I loved you when I first saw you. I loved you when your curiosity got the best of you and you finally spoke to me. I loved you when you would sneak out your window to come see me beneath the stars. I loved you when you didn't care that I was part wendigo. I loved you even though I believed you would never return my affections. I love you more than anything, Bea."

The corners of her lips curled up into a wide smile. "You're—" But then her elated expression fell when Heath started to fade and she remained the same. Beatrice grabbed him by the shoulders, her fingers digging in, begging him to take her with him. "Don't leave me here without you. Please."

"I wouldn't have spoken the words unless I truly believed you felt the same," Heath promised, his forefinger tilting her chin toward him. "You're not trapped here—I vow it. Just close your eyes and kiss me."

Beatrice grasped the sides of his face and captured his mouth with hers, tasting the coolness of a brisk autumn fall. Whether it failed or not, she repeated a soft incantation inside her head for them to remain together.

She broke the kiss and waited. Inside her chest, her heart came alive. *Thump-thump*. She inhaled, her lungs allowing her to breathe. Beneath her fingers she could still feel Heath's face, still feel his lingering touch on her hips. She slowly cracked open one eye, just in case he could easily vanish, yet he stood before her, only they were no longer ghostly entities but in *color*. Heath's curly blond hair, his eyes so deep brown they were almost black, sun-kissed tan skin, dark attire.

A forest of cherry blossom trees in the afterlife replaced the cemetery they'd been dancing in. Eventually she would explore her new world further, but for now, she wanted to stay here with Heath.

Beatrice's heart thrummed, and her breath hitched at his miraculous smile. "If I knew you fancied me," she said, "we could've been—"

"Kissing each other sooner." He winked.

"Yes!" Beatrice exclaimed, closing the distance between them. Heath's lips coasted across hers as he backed her against one of the flowering trees, their kisses as sweet as honey, his familiar amber scent enveloping her.

She remembered how he'd admitted to wanting to have done ungentlemanly things with her on the night they'd first gotten drunk on wine. It made her now want to do unladylike things with him here. "Let's teach one another how to make love," she uttered.

"That's your greatest idea thus far," he drawled.

With an elated grin, she helped him remove his coat, then untied his cravat before peeling his shirt over his head. Her pulse awakened even more when he slowly loosened the buttons at the back of her dress, one by one.

The fabric pooled into a heap at her feet, and she kicked it away like a pesky fly as her anticipation bloomed. Their gazes fastened on one another, his smile mirroring hers.

Beatrice arched a brow. "I think we have a corset to remove."

"Indeed we do."

Her corset was a tedious thing to get rid of, but after a few teasing moments, she was free of the cage. After what felt like a lifetime had trickled by, only bare flesh rested beneath their fingertips, waiting to be explored by one another.

Cheeks heating, butterflies swarming inside her, Beatrice slid her hand down Heath's chest, his muscled stomach, and finally between his legs. She drifted a finger up his sculpted length, finding it just as flawless as she imagined. Even though her strokes were clumsy at first, Heath groaned as if he'd been touched by a goddess.

His lips claimed hers, all consuming, before he trailed featherlight kisses across her jaw and down the crook of her neck. "I do believe it's my turn to touch you," he said gruffly.

"Please," she murmured.

Beatrice gasped when his hand grazed up her thigh, sending delicious tingles down her spine, and cupped her mound. His deft fingers dipped inside her heat as his palm pressed against her secret pearl. "You are exquisite," she breathed.

Heath continued to make her inner desires blossom until she begged for more. He cradled her in his arms, then sank down on a bed of leaves, allowing her to straddle his strong thighs. He flicked his tongue over a peaked nipple, making her back arch. Never had she imagined how good a man's hardness would feel against her softness. But oh, how heavenly it was when she instinctually rolled her hips forward, his length gliding up and down her center. Not a hint of shyness consumed her—because this was Heath, a man she trusted more than anyone.

Heath's lips returned to hers and their kisses deepened, growing greedy. With each taste of his tongue, her pulse hammered, wanting nothing more than for him to come even nearer.

He rolled Beatrice to her back, the bed of leaves akin to the softest of silks. "I'll try my damnedest to not ruin this, to make it last," Heath rasped.

"It will be perfect regardless." She cupped his face. "You know why? Because it's you and me, Heath."

Beatrice threaded her fingers in his soft hair and inhaled sharply as he buried himself inside her. No pain came as it would've if she'd been alive—only bliss. He moved gently, rhythmically, until delighted moans escaped her. As they grew more comfortable, Heath's pace picked up, his thrusts growing bolder. She held him tightly, and he brought one of her legs around his hips, allowing them further pleasure.

Her eyelids fluttered as a euphoric doorway opened, becoming purely spellful. Beatrice's heart thundered, her magic singing through her veins, building a wickedly wonderful heat that spread into every fiber of her being until a cry of pure joy slipped from her lips, her body humming with rapturous paradise.

Heath's movements turned wilder, her fingers digging into his firm buttocks. And then a deep groan barreled out of him as he discovered his own release, his body quaking beneath her touch. Her closest friend, her beautiful lover.

"I love you," she breathed as their chests heaved and their eyes met.

"I love you." He smiled, his lips caressing hers once more.

In between kisses, Beatrice yearned to uncover what other magical gratification they could offer one another. "And now," she purred, "will you make love to me like the couple we saw in the forest?"

A handsome smile lit up his entire face. "I am hopelessly under your charms, Bea. And for the rest of eternity, I promise you, I will never deny you anything."

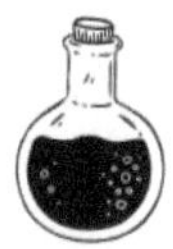

Did you enjoy Charmed by a Spell? Authors love reviews whether long or short!

Want more of the Headless Horseman? His story is coming soon in Bewitched by the Headless Horseman! Turn the page for a two-chapter sample.

Stevie Rourke is an ordinary ghost seer, minding her own business and thriving as a witch's assistant.

That is until the Eye of the Hollow opens and changes everything.

Now ghosts can see her, and even worse, the local psychopath, AKA the Headless Horseman, demands she help him.

As secrets of Sleepy Hollow begin to reveal themselves, Stevie learns she has no choice but to help the frustrating, albeit smoking hot, Horseman or watch her entire life fall into chaos.

BEWITCHED BY THE HEADLESS HORSEMAN

COMING AUGUST 2025

One ghost. Two ghosts. Three ghosts… No, wait, there's a fourth ghost. Oh, and now she's removing the guy's shirt. The guy ghost looked to be from somewhere in the early two-thousands with his emo band T-shirt and tight jeans, his hair shaggy and plastered over one eye, while the woman seemed to have possibly died during the 1800s. Which decade? That was anyone's guess. Her frilly black dress brushed her ankles, the collar high against her neck with a long strip of buttons.

And there goes her pristine bun. Oh, he's really going at it.

Stevie laughed under her breath—this was the

ultimate opposites attract. She sat outside the seafood restaurant on the second floor at a table for two, waiting on a supplier for the comic book store where she worked as her semi-sometimes job. Not only that though, the guy arriving just so happened to run one of the largest comic conventions in New York City each year. Her brother, Gideon, should've been at the restaurant for the meeting since the store was his after taking it over last year, but the torch had been passed to Stevie two months ago when he'd offered to give her two hundred dollars worth of vintage stamps along with regular pay. A deal she couldn't refuse, and after tonight, she would get those stamps to finish one of her bird collections. Owning antique things was a hobby she'd been clutching onto dearly for years.

She continued to observe the four translucent white ghosts around her. A loud bang struck the window in front of her, and her gaze locked onto the two ghosts who were getting mighty frisky on the opposite side of the glass. The woman's dress was now off somewhere on the floor, her body pressed to the window while a table of four steadily ate their meal, not noticing the action that was taking place before them. Their moans and groans were loud enough that Stevie was sure even ghosts lingering in the parking lot could hear them.

And there goes her corset. Stevie smirked to herself and flicked her stare away, not wanting to be too much of a peeper. But they were literally right there, her chair facing them!

She glanced at her phone, seeing Reese was already ten minutes late. Little monsters clawed at her stomach in nervousness—she'd made a grave mistake a few weeks ago when she'd snooped on the convention's website to reveal what he looked like after liking his witty back-and-forth emails. He was pretty much the spitting image of Evan Peters in *American Horror Story*—the *Coven* season. Hard to find a con there. She prayed it was one of those cases where the picture was better than the person so her fingers wouldn't fidget when he arrived.

Stevie set down her phone on the table and peered at one of the other two ghosts not getting freaky—a woman from possibly the 1950s with a tight polka-dotted bodice and a flowing black skirt, her hair in pinned curls. She weaved around the six outside tables in figure-eight movements, the click of her heels echoing, all while chattering to herself about the items she needed to buy at the grocery store. How humdrum. If the ghosts could see the living world, Stevie would've already coaxed the woman into the nearest grocery store and told her to have at it so her unfinished business could be checked off her list.

As she focused on her phone once again, Stevie's leg bounced up and down. *If he stands me up and Gideon doesn't give me those stamps, I swear I'll kidnap my brother's precious pet plant for a day or two*. She brought a piece of the complimentary bread to her mouth and chewed slowly while studying the one remaining ghost near the stone balcony. The one missing his head. *Poor sap*.

But it wasn't as if this was the first headless ghost she'd ever seen. When night gobbled up the day, a vengeful spirit, the Headless Horseman, rode his mighty steed through Sleepy Hollow and collected ghosts' heads. How often did he confiscate them? That was a really good question. And what he did with the heads? That was an even better question since every time she'd spotted him on horseback he was still headless. He probably added them to his secret stash or smugly fiddled around with them during the day when he wasn't out and about. If he ever found his original head, then maybe he would finally pass on and quit pestering the other ghosts. But with centuries having slipped by, his missing prize had to be long gone by now.

"After I finish this bite of bread, I'm leaving," she muttered, trying to ignore the woman's moans of ecstasy from inside the restaurant. Stevie had been seeing ghosts for as long as she could remember, most likely ever since she left the womb. No psychic abilities for her though—*too bad*. However, a seer's blood held magical properties such as necromancy and healing to name a couple. So at least she had that going for her.

"Stevie Rourke?" a melodious voice asked from behind her. She hurried and chewed the large piece of bread as her eyes locked onto dark brown irises, a pretty smile, and dirty blond curly hair brushing his brow. Reese wore a button-up shirt, the sleeves neatly at his wrists. Her stomach dipped at the sight of him. After the meeting she would throttle her sister-in-law, Lucia, for telling her he *so* didn't look like Evan Peters in person because he *so* did.

Stevie choked on her bread, looking like an idiot. She chugged half her glass of milk once she got the food down. "Sorry about that." She sobered and smiled, getting into non-seer mode by blocking out the surrounding ghosts since it would be an awkward first meeting otherwise. "Reese Braun?"

"That's me. Sorry I'm late. The traffic leaving the city was terrible." He raked a hand through his disheveled hair, his chest heaving and his cheeks flushed, while he sat across from her.

"No, it's fine," Stevie said just as a tall waitress came out to take their orders.

Lucia had given the green light that the meeting would be as easy as pie since Reese was a breeze for Gideon to deal with. Stevie's top priority job that she'd had for the past four years was working as a witch's assistant to Lucia. Running local deliveries for her around town and mailing out packages from the online side of Lucia's apothecary, other times assisting in mixing brews for her sister-in-law to spell. Pet plants and small skeletal animals for Sleepy Hollow locals were Lucia's specialty and best sellers, compliments of Stevie's seer blood added to help bring them to life of course.

When Stevie noticed she was staring at Reese's face like an owl, she chipped through the expanding iceberg. "So, about the booth and the auction—"

"The entrance booth is yours and you guys will have front row at the auction." The edges of Reese's lips curled up as he took a piece of bread and met her gaze.

"Oh." It was the only word Stevie could get out—she'd expected more of a challenge. But score.

The waitress returned with a green bottle and poured Reese a glass of red wine.

"You sure you don't want a glass?" he asked after she waved off the waitress from pouring her some.

"I'm a big milk drinker." Stevie winked, raising her glass like she was giving a toast and cursing herself once again for being an idiot.

"I like milk." Reese smiled, his teeth brilliantly white and perfectly straight. Her dentist father would be proud. "The meeting wasn't the only reason I came tonight though."

Stevie blinked, straightening in her seat. "It isn't? Then why?"

He leaned forward, his elbows resting on the table, appearing as if he were ready to spill a dark secret. "Don't take me for a stalker, but I looked up your picture on the store website and found you … cute."

Cute? No one had said anything like that to her since her ex-boyfriend. "I have a confession too. I tried looking up your picture on your website and you have an *anime* drawing."

Reese chuckled. "Kept you guessing, I hope."

"Terribly so." She bit her lip. "But then I went to the convention website and found your picture there."

His smile grew wide. "Should we call this a date then?"

Stevie cocked her head and grinned. "Guess my favorite color and we'll see if it is." She hadn't been on a date for nine months—ever since her one and only boyfriend dumped her just before her twenty-first birthday. Mister Piss-Baby, who shall not be named. They'd been together since high school, and one would *think* he'd have been used to the fact that Stevie could see the dead, but no. Every time he noticed her gaze drift from him to something he couldn't see, he'd gone pale as a corpse and she'd worried he would faint. Until finally he couldn't take it anymore. A reason she generally stayed hush-hush about her ability at first, especially if a boy claiming to love her couldn't handle it. Not that she'd broadcasted it before.

Reese tapped his hand against the table. "I'm debating between black like your dress or the same bright orange of your hair."

The headless ghost stumbled beside her table, then spun in circles. She didn't even break her act to look at him.

"Only one choice," Stevie finally said. To be fair, her favorite color was closer to a mood ring, and she enjoyed a good gothic dress, regardless of the color. But if she had to choose, it would be the orange he'd suspected which was why her hair had been the same color for the past six years.

"Maybe black," Reese said, taking a sip of his wine. "I've heard things about girls who wear lots of black."

She arched a brow. "What kind of things?"

"Oh shit, scratch that. Apparently, I can't be suave." He cringed.

Stevie placed her elbows on the table and steepled her fingers together. "No, do go on. You have my interest piqued."

"You know"—he cleared his throat—"that they are more adventurous."

She held back laughter, hoping he wasn't about to say what she was thinking. "Adventurous with what, Reese?"

He rolled his eyes, his cheeks reddening. "You know … in bed."

The laughter did come then and she couldn't stop it, even when it reached hyena levels. "I believe you're being prejudiced to the other colors."

"No, no, I didn't mean *you.* Your favorite color is orange." The red staining Reese's cheeks grew brighter and she covered her mouth to stop from laughing.

Still smiling, she said, "And what has he won for guessing the answer correctly, Mr. Gameshow Host? This is officially a date."

"You are—" Reese's phone dinged, and he fished it out from his pocket. "Fuck. That's my business partner. I need to meet with him about the convention before he royally screws up something else since he decided to get wasted. Again." He paused and kept his eyes trained on hers. "Maybe we can finish this official date soon?"

"If you want a part two, then there'll be a part two." At least she hoped he wanted to actually meet up again because she definitely did.

"We'll plan for a part two then. Oh, and Stevie, next time *you'll* have to guess my favorite color." Reese smiled brightly and drew out several bills to place on the table.

Stevie watched as he walked away, inwardly sighing that someone put together like him was interested in her. When the waitress brought Stevie the food, she stayed to polish off her meal—the untouched one she would drop off to Lucia.

Once the waitress gave her a to-go box, Stevie gathered her things, then walked by the headless ghost who now sat in one of the chairs at a table beside her. "You got this," she encouraged.

Stevie's cell beeped and Lucia was already messaging her.

Wishing you luck that the meeting goes well. You need to get some non-work-action after.

Stevie pinched the bridge of her nose and texted her back with a smile. *The only "some" I'll be getting tonight is some sleep. Reese got called into work, but tell Gideon he got the deal on both things. And by the way, he looks better than his picture by a long shot!*

I lied to you. He totally does.

You little witch! Lol.

Cauldron and all.

Anyway, I have food I'm going to drop off soon.

Stevie had known her sister-in-law for most of her life due to her mom's monthly visits to see Lucia's aunt Ginger for witchy remedies. Stevie had never been close with Lucia since they'd been six years apart, rarely even said hi to one another. All of that changed when Lucia started dating Gideon and asked Stevie to become a witch's assistant.

Stevie entered the restaurant and old twangy country music filled the crowded space. The two lovebird ghosts seemed to have taken their peepshow somewhere else.

She descended the wooden staircase, and at the bottom of the steps sat another ghost—a young girl maybe around eleven or twelve with thick white hair covering her face and knees. The girl's head lay in her hands as she cried. Some establishments didn't have any dead lingering while others were like a beacon to them. Even her brother's store had a resident ghost who'd been there for quite some time.

"I wish I could help you," Stevie murmured, knowing the ghost wouldn't hear her.

"No one can help me," the girl sobbed and stood, then ran through the wall like she was being chased by a wendigo wielding an axe.

Stevie's eyes widened, and she stumbled forward. Had the ghost heard her? No. Impossible. It had to have been a coincidence—it always was.

"Miss," the hostess called, drawing Stevie away from her thoughts. Bright cherry gloss stained the older woman's lips and her gray hair hung in a straight bob just past her chin. "The gentleman told me to give you this and to apologize again for his sudden departure." She then handed Stevie a pie box.

"Thank you." Stevie glanced down at the clear square top while heading toward the exit. An orange creamsicle pie rested inside and she pressed her lips together, fighting a smile when she read the words written in black ink on the edge of the box.

Sorry it's not your favorite shade of orange.

Stevie bit her lip—she loved orange creamsicle and would gladly eat the whole beautiful thing like a ravenous ogre.

As the crisp fall breeze hit her, Stevie stared up

at the night sky, the stars flickering like tiny watchful eyes. The new moon was somewhere up there, its silvery hue hidden, unable to cast its eerie glow down amongst the town of Sleepy Hollow.

Stevie took the path beside the woods, the restaurant not far from her home. The bushes beside her rustled, and she stopped in her tracks just as something that hadn't been alive in quite some time darted out from the tree line.

And ran straight toward her.

Stevie knelt against the cool pavement, a wide grin spreading her cheeks as she watched the white-furred animal barrel toward her. The fox barked in excitement while circling her, then leaped through her body. It was true that ghosts couldn't see Stevie, but it wasn't a fact that *all* ghosts couldn't. At some point in a seer's life, they were meant to have a ghost animal sidekick, AKA a familiar, who also held the ability to see both the living and the dead. A bouncy little fox she'd named Roxy had staked claim to her when a seven-year-old Stevie had been at the park with Gideon. Since then, the ghost was akin to a guardian.

"Did you really have to trail me here, Foxy Roxy?" Stevie's hand followed the curve of the ghost's form in an attempt to pet her sidekick. Her fingertips felt nothing but air, not even coldness or warmth surrounding the animal's essence.

Roxy sat on her haunches, her mouth pulled back into a smile, exposing her sharp teeth. The fox purred, swatting the air with her paw.

"Look, we're on what? Year fourteen here of knowing one another? In the next five years, I will make it a point for Lucia to figure out a spell so you'll feel me." Stevie laughed, passing her hand through the fox once more.

Roxy perked up, nudging her nose toward the pie box in Stevie's grasp.

"Oh, this?" She brought the box closer to the fox. "It's from my new friend. He knows how much I like orange."

The fox cocked her head, her ears perking straight up, wanting to hear more.

Even though there'd been a few friends by Stevie's side back in school, Roxy had always been the one she'd revealed her secrets to. "Right, so you know how I told you about Reese? It seems baby sparks might've flown. *Maybe.* But with my luck, he'll end up most likely becoming an acquaintance or someone I used to know. You know my history of keeping people around outside of family."

Roxy released a shrill bark, then took off into the

woods, disappearing behind the bushes and trees toward their neighborhood.

"I can't race you with this food in my hands or these stupid boots!" she shouted while smiling. "I'll see you soon!"

A young couple with their arms linked stared at Stevie curiously as they stepped around her. Stevie shrugged at them and gave her go-to response when someone caught what looked to be her talking to herself. "I'm just chatting to my other personality."

They nodded like it was no big deal and cuddled each other closer before crossing the street. The people of Sleepy Hollow were used to a good number of residents holding some sort of supernatural ability, usually witchy. Some outsiders would consider them cursed, while others would shout from the rooftops that they were blessed. Stevie's mom once believed herself to be cursed, but after coming to Sleepy Hollow well before popping out Gideon and Stevie, her ability proved to be, while not quite a blessing, at least an unfortunate ailment that could be maintained. Anyone who lived in the town, regardless if they were paranormal-less, knew to keep Sleepy Hollow's secrets sealed behind tightened lips to outsiders or face the council's wrath.

Stevie resumed her walk home down the pavement since going through the darkened woods would be nothing but a hazard—she didn't have

Roxy's superhero eyesight. As a gust of chilly air ruffled her orange locks and tickled her skin, she cursed herself for not bringing a sweater.

Up ahead, in the middle of the street, a white translucent form shook his fist in the air. "Where is my fucking car?" the young guy screamed, his short hair stuck up around his head like a mad scientist. His suit looked like it was straight out of an old seventies catalog with bell-bottom pants and a button-up shirt tucked into the waist.

"It's long gone now, buddy," she hollered.

The ghost glanced her way, his lips twisted into a snarl as he yelled, "It isn't. It's coming this way, missy."

Stevie stilled, sucking in a sharp breath, her lungs tight while her gaze glued to the back of his head. This was *not* a coincidence. He'd *heard* her, *seen* her. She'd chalked up the girl at the restaurant as nothing, but it had been *something*. Unless … he'd been a seer before he'd died and the other ghost at the restaurant really hadn't seen her.

Stevie peered up toward the star-filled sky, where the new moon should've been. A cloud drifted toward the west, revealing a flash of red and she gasped. *No way*. It couldn't finally be … but it was! Giddiness seeped further toward her bones with each pound of her heart. The *Eye* of Sleepy Hollow had opened!

A story had been passed down from generation

to generation that one day—no one knew when—two magical new moons would fall a cycle apart. During the first new moon, one Eye of the Hollow would open, and the dead would see the living. It was said that for an entire month the veil over the departed would remain lifted, until the following new moon when the second Eye opened and all the living would see the dead for a single night before the Eyes sealed once again, separating the two worlds.

Stevie cupped her hands around her mouth like a megaphone. "So you can see me?"

The ghost scowled at her. "Of course I can. We knew this day would eventually come. It's a fucking curse I can't return to not seeing you, though," he grumbled just as a car came around the curve and passed through him.

Well, then… "I was going to see if you needed help with any unfinished business, but since you have the most *wonderful* attitude I've ever come across, you can figure it out yourself."

"I don't give a fuck about that," he grunted and flipped her the bird, then chose to ignore her.

"Good luck to you then," Stevie sang.

"He's a fool. Ignore him," a female voice said from behind Stevie, her small form hidden behind a tree a few feet away. The ghost was maybe in her forties, her hair in a long braid down one of her shoulders, and an ill-fitted dress dwarfed her body.

Stevie stepped toward the woman. "Not that I can for sure complete your unfinished business, but do you need anything?"

"No thank you." The woman shrugged. "I'm waiting until after the second Eye opens. I want to tell my daughter I'm sorry. That's my unfinished business. It's a shame that a lot of the ghosts are trapped inside their own minds, believing they are still alive or already in Heaven or the Hollow. With the Eye open now, some will continue to not see what's right in front of them."

The Hollow was really what Hell was to outsiders, only the fiendish things that were down there were far worse than any book or movie had ever described. Demons in the Hollow could shift into any horrific creature they wished.

"That's good she's still here for you to find." For others who'd died longer ago, they wouldn't be so lucky. But on the bright side, they could possibly meet up with another blood relative.

Stevie studied the Eye of the Hollow, the night surrounding the town, knowing the Headless Horseman would slither out sometime soon since darkness was here. As though her thoughts had summoned the psychopath, a horse's hooves pounded in the distance, the ominous sound filling the air. Since everyone drove cars these days, she couldn't chalk it up to just any rando horse, not in this tech-driven century. The bridge was just across the street, and the hoofbeats of the horse picked up, thumping across the earth.

"Go!" the woman slipped from behind the tree, shouting at the ghost still standing in the middle of the road.

"Yeah, you don't want to be caught up in that maniac's head-stealing game," Stevie added half-heartedly since he'd been a dick.

She stepped back into the foliage, listening to the hoofbeats slowing against wooden planks, becoming measured when the vengeful spirit broke out from the enclosure of the bridge, appearing in all his narcissistic glory as his cape billowed behind him. The Headless Horseman and his stallion were both the same translucent shade of white as every other ghost, not swathed in black as memorabilia liked to show. The only colorful thing about him was the glowing orange jack-o'-lantern in his gloved right hand. A sword hung at his hip, and Stevie couldn't pinpoint exactly how he could see or hear without a head. It had to be the vibrations which was why the jerkwad in the road needed to remain still. Even then, without a brain, how could the Horseman think? Or did the stallion just guide him to pluck a toy of his choice? Unless the pumpkin's cut-out eyes were like his own? Stevie was leaning toward the second option.

But before she could think on it more, the ghost in the road seethed at the Horseman, "Ah, fuck you, asshole."

The Horseman sat taller, his shoulders squaring as the stallion turned to face the idiot. Puffs of air escaped the horse's nostrils, and brilliant white eyes glowed bright while it focused on the Horseman's prey.

Stevie gazed at the scene, unable to turn away. "This point now goes to the Headless Horseman," she whispered to the woman.

"You should leave," the woman stuttered, her body trembling while creeping toward the darkness of the woods.

Stevie didn't need to be as wary as this woman. First, Stevie wasn't a ghost, so he couldn't just choose her head for the picking. And second, that was it. She'd never seen firsthand a head taken by the Horseman before. Only caught sight of him galloping through the streets when she'd been driving to or from somewhere at night.

The horse whinnied, and Stevie craned her neck to get a better view as the psychopath hopped down from his stallion, the sound of his boots against gravel crunching. Her gaze raked down his muscular form, and she set the thought on fire that his body looked *good.*

As he edged toward the ghost, it was like a scene from a movie, the anticipation, the wondering which direction this would play out even though she had a pretty decent hunch. If there was a bowl of popcorn beside her, she would've been reaching for it as she watched on.

The Horseman lifted his pumpkin, his bicep flexing beneath his tight shirt, while the other ghost flipped him the middle finger the way he had at Stevie. Taking a cocky step forward, the Horseman hurled the flaming jack-o'-lantern at the ghost's chest. The guy stilled, his body frozen, his coloring changing from ivory to orange like flickering embers.

The Horseman effortlessly freed his sword from the sheath at his hip. With one fatal swing, he sliced it clean through the ghost's neck. No scream. No blood. Nothing. *Not gruesome at all, to be honest.* The Horseman reached into the ghost's chest and ripped out his pumpkin. He then picked up his prized head from the ground before placing it on his own neck.

"Real tough guy," Stevie muttered under her breath as she stepped back onto the pavement to get to her house.

The Horseman whirled around, the head he'd just placed on his neck no longer there, seeming to have vanished. *What in all the witchy magic?* He faced her, and she blinked, realizing that even though he was without a head again, he could sense her, possibly somehow hear and see her, since the Eye was open.

"He's such a tough guy that he stood me up for our date," Stevie rambled while fishing out her phone from her purse and walking at a normal pace, pretending as though she was like the general public, unable to see ghosts. "This world sucks sometimes. Sucks the life right out of people." *Unless they're taking heads instead of sucking.* The Horseman's boots didn't crunch across the gravel, nor did his stallion's hooves. Yet she could feel them both watching her.

Trying to appear casual, she whistled to herself as if she didn't notice he was somewhere behind her being his head-stealing self.

And so what if he could notice her? It wasn't like he could touch her and rip her head off for himself. Her head would remain happily in place.

Yet she still didn't want him to follow her home and get stuck with a demonic spirit who was akin to something that would come straight from the Hollow. As she turned the corner, she lost her cool and took off running in case he decided to tag along. Her boots weighed her down, and she stumbled, but it didn't stop her from hurrying to the duplex on the next street.

Roxy stood outside Stevie's door on all fours, wagging her fluffy tail.

Stevie drank in deep breath after deep breath, her chest heaving, perspiration dripping down the back of her neck. "Looks like you beat me again. Sorry it took me so long. I got caught up with Sleepy Hollow's nightly *guest*."

Stevie's phone dinged, and she glanced at the

screen. Reese. The edges of her lips curled up.

Just wanted to say you're even cuter in person, and I can't wait to see you again.

Likewise. And thank you for the pie. I'm not sharing it with anyone.

On part two of our date we can share something else then.

Stevie arched a brow. A tap came at the window of the other half of the duplex, startling her. She rolled her eyes when she found Lucia waving from her and Gideon's bedroom. Her sister-in-law lived on one side of the duplex and Stevie on the other. With the rent being cheaper this way, she'd been able to move out of her parents' house a couple of weeks ago. Finally.

"Delivery." Stevie shook the bag in front of Lucia. "And apparently the Eye of the Hollow is *alive*."

Lucia's gaze widened and Stevie waited a few seconds for her to open the door. She stood in nothing but an oversized Wolverine T-shirt that fell just above her knees. Her jet-black hair was thrown up into a messy bun on top of her head.

"The Eye opened?" Lucia gasped, taking the bag from Stevie while staring up at the red glowing spot above them. "Witch's tits! I wasn't expecting it to happen in our lifetime."

"That's not all. I left the restaurant and crossed paths with Mr. No Good, and—" Hoofbeats piercing the neighborhood reverberated around them, and Stevie clutched the pie box tighter.

"Seriously? He's like a vulture you can't get rid of." Stevie grasped her sister-in-law by the arm and pulled Lucia inside the duplex. She slammed the door shut and locked it. Roxy was already behind them, silent, looking toward the window.

"What is it?" Lucia asked.

"Shh!" She put her finger over her lips. "The Headless Horseman is coming."

Lucia arched a brow. "I didn't need the quiet signal."

Stevie held her breath until the hoofbeats picked up and faded before releasing a sigh. It wasn't abnormal to hear the stallion as she'd heard him over the years riding up and down the streets. But just in case, it was better they weren't in the same proximity again.

Lucia set the bag of food on the floor and placed her hands on her hips. "Can we talk now?" she whispered. "I only feel Roxy's presence." Besides being one of the most powerful witches in Sleepy Hollow, a little psychic ability pulsed within Lucia's blood. But she couldn't see the ghosts the way Stevie could.

"His Headlessness is gone." Stevie angled her neck to peek inside the empty bedroom. "Where's Gideon?"

Lucia batted her hand behind her. "In the living room playing his new video game with his headphones on."

"We could be getting our souls sucked out by a band of demons and he wouldn't hear a thing." Stevie rolled her eyes. "As I was saying before we were rudely interrupted, the Eye is open and I can talk to the dead now."

Lucia rubbed her chin. "Hmm. Not much different than in the movies for a seer then."

"I'm waiting for you, Lucia," Gideon purred, his annoying voice drifting down the hallway. "The game's done, I put Maxine in the kitchen, and I'm undressed." Maxine was Gideon's plant that resembled a cross between a Venus flytrap, the one in *Little Shop of Horrors*, and the snapping flowers from the Super Mario video games. Lucia had given the plant to Gideon as an anniversary gift one year, and he'd babied it ever since.

"Be there in a minute. Just telling your sister goodnight," Lucia yelled over her shoulder as Stevie wrinkled her nose.

"And you owe me stamps!" Stevie added.

A couple of grumbled curses came from the living room.

"I'll let you get to *that*," Stevie said to Lucia, "and we can discuss more tomorrow."

"That we will do. The owner did bless the house recently, but I'll put up some stronger wards tomorrow."

"I'm glad to have my own personal witch next

door." Stevie smiled, cracking open her exit, then bolting inside her half of the house. The pie rattled again, most likely crumbs by now, but still devourable.

As she locked up for the night, a thought struck her. *If the heads vanish when the Headless Horseman puts them on, then where do they go?*

Stevie shrugged and looked down at her pie—somewhat intact. "Time for a much-needed dessert after this night." She held up the box in a toast. "To the next thirty days and helping any ghost who asks for my assistance."

ALSO FROM CANDACE ROBINSON

Wicked Souls Duology
Vault of Glass
Bride of Glass

Marked by Magic
The Bone Valley
Merciless Stars

Cruel Curses Trilogy
Clouded By Envy
Veiled By Desire
Shadowed By Despair

Untamed Darkness Series
Dearest Clementine
These Vicious Thorns
Savage Delights
And Then There Was Silence
Her Cruel Dahlias

Cursed Hearts Duology
Lyrics & Curses
Music & Mirrors

Between the Quiet
Hearts Are Like Balloons
Bacon Pie

Avocado Bliss

Faeries of Oz Series

Lion (Short Story Prequel)

Tin

Crow

Ozma

Tik-Tok

Vampires in Wonderland Series

Rav (Short Story Prequel)

Maddie

Chess

Knave

Once Upon A Wicked Villain

Spindle of Sin

Acknowledgments

So, I've been wanting to write a short paranormal historical romance that involved friends to lovers. That story led me to put it in Sleepy Hollow! So thank you, dear readers, for taking a chance on this one.

There are some wonderful people who have helped with book after book, and I appreciate it with all my heart. Amber H. is the spell working fixes guru! S.G.D. performs magic on the story! And to Hayley, Jolene, Jerica, and Ann, you guys are positively charming with proofreading!

To my family and friends, thank you for keeping me going each day.

If you'd like to know more about the Headless Horseman, fear not, he'll be in the next book, Bewitched by the Headless Horseman. For now, Beatrice and Heath still dance together every night.

About the Author

Candace Robinson spends her days consumed by words and hoping to one day find her own DeLorean time machine. Her life consists of avoiding migraines, admiring Bonsai trees, watching classic movies, and living with her husband and daughter in Texas—where it can be forty degrees one day and eighty the next.

www.ingramcontent.com/pod-product-compliance
Lightning Source LLC
Chambersburg PA
CBHW030601310726
48979CB00003B/530
* 9 7 8 1 9 6 0 9 4 9 4 8 6 *